For Heidi, who gives me the gift of amazing editing!
Merry Christmas!
—B.C.S.

For Kate and Nate
—C.S.

Text copyright © 2018 by Brianna Caplan Sayres
Jacket art and interior illustrations copyright © 2018 by Christian Slade

All rights reserved. Published in the United States by Random House Children's Books, a division of Penguin Random House LLC, New York.

Random House and the colophon are registered trademarks of Penguin Random House LLC.

Visit us on the Web! rhcbooks.com

Educators and librarians, for a variety of teaching tools, visit us at RHTeachersLibrarians.com

Library of Congress Cataloging-in-Publication Data
Names: Sayres, Brianna Caplan, author. | Slade, Christian, illustrator.
Title: Where do diggers celebrate Christmas? / Brianna Caplan Sayres ; illustrated by Christian Slade.
Description: New York : Random House Books for Young Readers, 2018. |
Summary: "A picture book that showcases all kinds of vehicles celebrating the Christmas holiday" —Provided by publisher.
Identifiers: LCCN 2018005298 (print) | LCCN 2018013386 (ebook) |
ISBN 978-1-5247-7215-4 (hardback) | ISBN 978-1-5247-7216-1 (hardcover library binding) | ISBN 978-1-5247-7217-8 (ebook)
Subjects: | CYAC: Stories in rhyme. | Vehicles—Fiction. | Christmas—Fiction. | BISAC: JUVENILE FICTION / Transportation / Cars & Trucks. |
JUVENILE FICTION / Bedtime & Dreams. | JUVENILE FICTION / Holidays & Celebrations / Christmas & Advent.
Classification: LCC PZ8.3.S274 (ebook) | LCC PZ8.3.S274 Wf 2018 (print) |
DDC [E]—dc23

MANUFACTURED IN CHINA
10 9 8 7 6 5 4 3 2 1
First Edition

Where Do Diggers Celebrate Christmas?

by Brianna Caplan Sayres · illustrated by Christian Slade

Random House 🏠 New York

Where do diggers spend Christmas
after all their excavation?
Do they dig a giant Christmas tree
for their family's celebration?

Where do cherry pickers celebrate
once they've stretched to reach great heights?
Do they hang up strings of colored bulbs
that make truck stops bright with lights?

Where do forklifts spend Christmas
after lifting up big barrels?
Do they carry loads of presents,
then sing fun Christmas carols?

Where do mixers celebrate Christmas
after a day of highway fixing?
Do they gather with their families
for some yummy eggnog mixing?

Where do cranes celebrate Christmas when they've lifted loads high and low? Do they share their Christmas spirit beneath the mistletoe?

Where do tanker trucks celebrate
when they've filled up at the dairy?
Do they serve up milk and cookies
to make Santa's Christmas merry?

Where do tow trucks spend Christmas
after towing cars all day?
Do they trade places with the reindeer
to help Santa pull his sleigh?

Where do tractors celebrate Christmas
after plowing row by row?
Do they gather by a manger
for their annual Christmas show?

Where do food trucks celebrate Christmas
after serving lots of meals?
Are there special Christmas menus
at these restaurants on wheels?

Where do Zambonis spend Christmas
after all the ice is clear?
Do they skate across a frozen lake,
spreading Christmas cheer?

Where do all these trucks celebrate?
Is it at a construction site?
Do they beep their horns to "Jingle Bells"
for a not-so-silent night?

Do they hang their Christmas ornaments?
Do they watch the *Truckcracker* ballet?
Do they visit Grandma and Grandpa Truck
for a perfect Christmas Day?

Where do your trucks celebrate Christmas
when those sleigh bells start to jingle?
They'll be waiting under the Christmas tree
for their visit from old Kris Kringle!